RUSS THOMPSON

CANS

Finding Forward

Books

Published by Finding Forward Books
P.O. Box 8182, Long Beach, CA 90808
www.findingforwardbooks.com

Editing by Laura Perkins. Series concept by Pam Sheppard. Text set in Open Dyslexic Mono.

Library of Congress Control No.: 2023922330
ISBN: 979-8-9890657-4-5 (paperback)
ISBN: 979-8-9890657-5-2 (ebook)
FILE: FF008-25C-2025-03-08

Summary: A teen who dreams of attending college must fight to overcome the effects of poverty.

BISAC Subject Codes: YOUNG ADULT FICTION / Social Themes / Class Differences | YOUNG ADULT FICTION / Social Themes / Emotions and Feelings

Lexile readability measure: HL540L

For Betty Jean,
our kids,
and grandkids.

CONTENTS

1 CANS

AFTER MIDNIGHT. I like to drive. But I hate driving this old truck.

The side is smashed in, the back is rusted out, and the engine runs bad.

We cross under the train bridge to the good side of town.

I look sideways at Dad.

He's dead tired from working all day. And the bandage covering his right hand is filthy.

But he never complains.

I turn left onto Orchard Avenue.

All of the houses are perfect. It's like one of those rich neighborhoods in the movies.

But trash day is tomorrow, so the bins are out on the street.

"Gilbert," says Dad. "Let's start here."

I pull to the curb, put on my headlamp, and get out.

Dad slides behind the wheel.

He's not supposed to drive with the infection in his hand. But we don't have a choice.

I get to the first house and open the recycling bin. There's nothing, just paper and cardboard.

The bin at the next house is better. It has about fifty soda cans. I reach in, pull them out, and put them in my trash bag.

Next, I get to The Castle, the

biggest house in Conroy.

There's a bicycle parked in front with a sign that says FREE.

It's a beach bike with a coaster brake, the kind that would be just right for Billy.

The only thing wrong with it, is that it has a flat tire.

I signal Dad. He brings the truck up. I put the bike in the back.

I wish we could keep it.

But I know we can't.

I walk to the next house with Dad following me.

TWO IN THE MORNING. Time to go home.

Dad pulls over and stops the engine.

I get in the driver's seat, restart the truck, and pull away from the curb.

Five minutes later, we cross
under the train bridge.
It's been a good night.
We got a bike, a microwave, and
four bags of cans.

2 THE GRADES I GET

TUESDAY MORNING. I sit at the kitchen table and wish I could have slept longer.

Mom sits across from me in her faded bathrobe. "Gilbert, you look worn out," she says.

I see the look in her eyes. She's tired, too.

I look around the kitchen.

Everything is scrubbed clean. But the floor tiles under the sink are cracked. And two of the burners on the stove don't work. Our whole house is like that.

"Mom, is it true that Mr. Willis is going to raise our rent again?"

"It's true," she says. "Dad talked to him yesterday. It didn't do any good."

I see the worried look on her face. It scares me.

"But I think we might be okay," she says. "I should be getting a raise next month."

I know she means well. But that's what she said last month.

I pour a bowl of cereal. The milk is gone again. I'll have to eat it dry.

SEVEN-FIFTEEN. Time to leave for school. Cousin Billy and I walk down the driveway.

We pass Dad's truck with the bike

in the back.

I hope Billy doesn't notice it. I should have put it in the garage when we came home last night.

We reach the sidewalk and turn right. The first stop will be Keller Middle School.

"That's... a... nice... bike... in... your... dad's... truck," Billy says.

"We got lucky," I say. "Dad thinks he can sell it for a lot."

"That's... good," Billy says. "I... know... it... will... help."

I see the hurt in his eyes. I know he wishes he could have it. We all do.

Billy and I keep walking. It's not long before we cross under the train bridge.

Three blocks later, we're at

Keller Middle School.

I wait on the sidewalk and watch as he goes up the front steps. His limp is almost gone.

It's been eight months since the car accident.

His mom and dad were killed. And he's still recovering from his skull fracture.

But he never complains.

And he never gives up.

I wish things weren't so hard for him.

EDISON HIGH SCHOOL. Every time I walk through the front gate, I feel like I don't belong.

All of the kids come from rich families. And they all think they're better than me.

I turn left to go to my locker.

There she is, Fiona.

She may be rich, but she's also nice.

She doesn't look down on me like the other kids do.

FOOD COURT. School starts in twenty minutes. I sit with Darrell at our table in the back.

He always wears a collar shirt to look preppy. But everybody knows we come from the other side of the train bridge.

"Gilbert, how come you're yawning?" he asks.

We've been friends for a long time. But I would never tell him what Dad and I do at night.

"I stayed up late to study," I say. "Are you ready for the quiz in statistics?"

　　"I looked at the review sheet,"
he says. "I think I'll be fine."
　　What he really means is that
he'll probably get an A.
　　School is easy for him.
　　But I have to work for the grades
I get.

3 CAN'T SLEEP

ECONOMICS CLASS. This is our day to write essays. Mr. Rubio comes to the front of the room and points to the whiteboard.

"The topic for today is about real life," he says. "I want you to write about how you will handle your money after you graduate this spring. Use your best thinking. You get twenty minutes."

It's something I hate to think about. But I begin writing.

Gilbert Neely
Economics, Period 1
Mr. Rubio

Money and College

When I look ahead to next year, I don't know what's going to happen. I want to go to college. But things keep going wrong.

My dad went straight to work when he left high school. He has always worked two jobs. But he doesn't make very much.

When you wash dishes and clear tables in a restaurant, there's not much money in that.

When you clean offices, there's not much money in that, either.

And when you lose both jobs because the economy goes bad, what *do you do?*

My mom works as a secretary at a trucking company. She would like to be a manager. But since she didn't go to college, there's only so far she can go.

I would like to go to Raymond State College. That would be my dream.

After that, I want to be a teacher.

But to do that, I have to get a scholarship.

And to get a scholarship, I have to get good grades.

But my grades have been going down because I'm working all the time.

It's like my dream of going to college is slipping away from me.

TWENTY MINUTES LATER. Mr. Rubio comes to the front of the room.

"Time is up," he says. "Hand in your papers."

I pass up my essay and look around the room.

Darrell will be going to college. He has a chance for a scholarship. And he doesn't have to work to support his family.

Fiona will also be going. She's one of the smartest people in the school. And I'm sure her family has lots of money.

I look again at Mr. Rubio.

"The important thing to remember is that you can all achieve your dreams." he says. "If somebody else can do it, you can do it too."

It sounds good. And I want to believe him. But everything keeps going wrong for me.

I think about the HELP WANTED sign I saw at Burger House.

Maybe I could work there after school and still help Dad at night.

I put my head down to rest my eyes for a minute.

Somebody shakes my shoulder.

"Gilbert, wake up," Mr. Rubio says. "The bell rang."

Fiona smiles at me.

I feel stupid because she saw me sleeping.

I pick up my books and pretend not to notice her.

I wish I wasn't so tired all the time.

LUNCH. I sit across the table from Darrell and take out my sandwich.

"Are you going on the trip to

Raymond State this Saturday?" he asks.

"I'd like to. But I have to do my lawn jobs."

"That's a drag," he says. "It seems like all you do is work."

He's right. But we need the money.

AFTER SCHOOL. Home. I go to my room, flop on my bed, and close my eyes to get some sleep.

But I can't.

Mom and Dad are arguing again. I hear them through the wall.

"You can't keep doing this to him," Mom says. "He's tired all the time. It's starting to affect his schoolwork."

"I know it's tough for him," Dad says. "But we don't have a choice.

We're about an inch away from getting evicted."

I'm glad when their voices get quieter.

But I still can't sleep.

4 STAY WITH ME

DINNER. I go out to the kitchen. Mom, Dad, and Billy are already at the table.

I feel better after getting some rest. I dish up some spaghetti from the stove and sit down.

"Gilbert, I got a call from Mr. Rubio," Mom says. "He told me you fell asleep in class today."

"It was only for a minute," I say. "The room was hot."

Mom glares at Dad.

Dad glares back.

I don't want them to fight. Maybe I can change the subject.

"Dad, how's your hand?" I ask.

"They packed it again and put on a new dressing," he says. "They also gave me a different antibiotic."

"You're also supposed to take it easy," Mom says.

"That's true," says Dad. "We also have bills to pay."

Mom's jaw tightens. Her face turns red.

Dad slides his chair back and takes a deep breath. "I have to go out and check on something."

He gets up from the table, rinses his plate in the sink, and steps out the back door.

Billy and I finish eating.

We know not to say anything.

AFTER DINNER. I sit at the kitchen table and open the laptop. It's old, and the case is cracked. But it works.

Billy sits across from me. He reads from one of the books his teacher gave him.

I watch as he runs his finger under the words and moves his lips.

I feel bad for him. But he never quits trying.

I get on the Khan Academy for my statistics class.

It's hard for me to understand the textbook. And sometimes Mr. Braden is confusing. But the Khan guy explains it in a way that makes everything seem simple.

I finish the section, take the test, and get everything right.

Economics is next. But I'm tired.

I get up and make myself another cup of coffee.

I have to stay awake.

BEDROOM. Dark. Dad shakes my shoulder.

My clock says midnight. Billy is sleeping. I have to be quiet.

I get out of bed, get dressed, grab my shoes, and go out to the living room.

Dad gives me a cup of coffee. I finish it and put on my shoes. We're ready.

We go out to the truck. I get in the driver's seat and turn the key. Nothing happens, just clicking.

"Sounds like the battery," Dad says.

I get the jumper cables and open the truck hood.

Dad pulls up in Mom's car. We connect the cables.

I get in the truck and turn the key. It starts.

"We'll have to keep the motor running tonight," Dad says. "I don't want to get stuck somewhere."

TWO IN THE MORNING. It's been a good night. We got five bags of cans and an aluminum barbecue.

We reach the last house on Glendon Street.

Dad pulls up next to me. "Let's call it a night," he says.

He keeps the motor running and slides over to the passenger side.

"I'm still worried about the battery," he says. "Don't let the engine stall."

I climb in, get behind the wheel,

and put it in drive.

The engine slows.

I tap the gas.

Nothing happens.

I push harder.

We zoom forward.

Tree ahead.

Bang!

Flashing lights.

Paramedics.

Siren.

Head hurts.

Dad yelling. "Keep your eyes open. We're almost to the hospital. Stay with me."

5 CAN'T WORK

HEAD HURTS. Won't stop.

Voices.

Hallway.

Lights.

Lady, scratchy voice.

"Gilbert, can you hear me?"

"Where am I?"

"I'm Dr. Fox. You're at the hospital. We're going to take care of you."

"Who are you?"

"I'm a doctor. We're going to help you."

"Where am I?"

"You're at the hospital."

"Who are you?"

"I'm the doctor."

"My head hurts."

BLURRY. Shouting. Lights. Bright.

"Where am I?"

Mom's voice. "Gilbert, you're in
the emergency room."

"What happened?"

"You hit your head. The
paramedics brought you here."

"Why am I here?"

Dad's voice. "You crashed the
truck into a tree."

"What tree?"

Lady. White coat. "Gilbert, do
you remember me?"

"Who are you?"

"I'm Dr. Fox. I got the results

of your CT scan. Everything looks
good."

Mom. "What does that mean?"

Doctor. "There are no fractures.
But I want him to stay one more
night to be sure everything is
okay."

I look around. "What happened to
me?"

Doctor. "You have a grade-three
concussion."

I feel the bandage on my head.
"What's this for?"

Dad. "You cut your head."

"How?"

Doctor. "You need to rest."

My head spins. I want it to stop.

HOSPITAL ROOM. It's quiet now.

Mom, Dad, and Billy look down at
me.

"How are you feeling?" Mom asks.

"What happened?" I ask.

"You... didn't... put... on... your... seatbelt," Billy says. "Your... head... hit... the... steering... wheel."

He squeezes my hand. I see tears in his eyes.

I think about the accident where his parents died. I think about his skull fracture.

I feel lucky.

"How is the truck?" I ask Dad.

"The front is smashed in pretty bad," he says. "But I think I can fix it. I'm going to pound out the dents and put in a new radiator."

"Gilbert, try not to worry about the truck," Mom says. "The main thing is for you to get better."

HOSPITAL ROOM. Night.

Dad sleeps in the chair next to me. Mom and Billy are gone.

My head feels better.

But I wrecked the truck.

And without the truck, Dad can't work.

6 ONE WEEK LATER

FRIDAY MORNING. Edison High School. I enter the front gate.

It's good to be back. But I'm a week behind in everything. It will be hard to catch up, especially in statistics.

I walk to the food court and sit across from Darrell.

"Gilbert, how's your head?" he asks.

"Pretty good. The stitches come out tomorrow."

"What about your dad's truck?"

"He's still working on it."

"Don't you have insurance?" he asks.

"The guy who hit us didn't have any. My dad decided to fix it himself."

I don't like lying.

The truth is that we don't have car insurance.

But nobody outside our family needs to know that.

ECONOMICS. Fiona smiles at me when I sit down.

It always surprises me when she's nice to me.

Mr. Rubio walks around the room and hands back papers. He gives me my test from a week ago.

It's a C. I remember when I only used to get A's and B's.

"Glad to see you back," Mr. Rubio
says. "What happened?"

"We were hit by a car. I got a
concussion."

"I'm glad you came through it
okay," he says. "We missed you."

It seems strange to hear him say
that. I didn't think he noticed me
that much.

He steps to the front of the
classroom. "Open your books to page
eighty-two. This is about prices and
markets. Read to page eighty-six.
When you finish, you will discuss it
with your elbow partner."

I begin reading. It's
complicated, but I understand it.

Ten minutes pass. Mr. Rubio comes
to the front of the classroom. "Get
with your elbow partner and discuss
the reading. You get eight minutes."

My elbow partner is Fiona. We
slide our desks together.

"I'm sorry about your accident,"
she says. "I saw it when they put
you into the ambulance. I was
worried."

"What do you mean?"

"It was our tree that you hit."

A cold feeling comes over me. I
look around the room.

I hope she didn't tell anybody.

DINNER. I sit at the kitchen table
with Mom, Dad, and Billy.

Dad has alcohol on his breath. I
act like I don't notice.

"Gilbert, I finished fixing the
truck today," he says. "We can go
out tonight."

Mom's jaw drops. "But we talked
about it. You said he wouldn't be

going out with you."

"I thought about it again," Dad says. "We don't have a choice. And it's only until my hand gets better."

Mom glares at him.

Dad goes to the sink, rinses off his plate, and walks out the back door to the garage.

I don't want to go out with him.

But we need the money.

EVENING. Billy and I do our homework at the kitchen table.

Billy whispers to me. "I... went... out... to... the... garage... Your... dad... was... drinking... He... put... away... the... bottle... when... he... saw... me."

I've known for a while that Dad

was drinking again.

And his hand should have healed by now.

It was six weeks ago when he cut it.

7 LONG TIME

MIDNIGHT. Dad opens the gate to the street. I buckle my seatbelt, start the truck, and pull out of the driveway.

Dad gets in and closes the door. I'm glad I don't smell alcohol on his breath.

"Gilbert, the battery I got from the junkyard should be okay," he says. "But I need you to keep the motor running, just in case."

It makes me nervous about keeping the motor running. But we can't let the engine stall.

I turn left onto Cabot Street.
The front end of the truck shakes as
soon as I get above thirty-five
miles an hour.

"Just keep it slow," Dad says. "I
couldn't fix the front suspension."

I slow down to thirty and grip
the steering wheel hard to keep us
going straight.

The truck stops shaking. I feel
better. We pass under the train
bridge to the good side of town.

"Dad, thanks for taking my lawn
jobs tomorrow," I say.

"Billy will be with me, so it
should be okay," Dad says. "Where's
your field trip?"

"Munson State. It's where Mr.
Kennison went."

"Who's that?"

"He's my journalism teacher. He's
also the one taking us on the trip.
He asked me to write about it for
the school newspaper."

We hit a bump. The front of the
truck shakes again.

I hold the wheel tighter and slow
down more.

I'll be glad when we get home.

TWO IN THE MORNING. It's been a good
night. We have six bags of cans in
the back.

Dad pulls over, puts the truck in
park, and keeps the engine running.

I get in, buckle my seatbelt, put
the truck in drive, and pull away
from the curb with no problems.

Ten minutes later, we're almost
to the train bridge.

"Gilbert, look behind you," Dad

says.

A police car comes up behind us with its red lights flashing. I grip the steering wheel harder.

It passes and keeps going.

"Remember what to do if you ever get pulled over," Dad says. "Turn on the interior light, put your hands on the wheel, and do whatever the officer tells you."

He's said this a thousand times. I remember when he told me about how he was arrested for drunk driving.

He had tears in his eyes. He told me not to be like him.

It reminds me of when I found out that he couldn't read.

He tries to hide it.

But I've known for a long time.

8 DON'T THINK

SATURDAY MORNING. The sun shines
into my room.

I'm tired. But I'm excited.

I go on the field trip to Munson
State today.

I know I can't go to school
there.

But it will be fun to see the
campus.

KITCHEN. I sit down and pour a bowl
of cereal.

Mom and Billy are already eating.

But something is wrong.

"Where's Dad?" I ask.

Mom looks up. She's worn out. "I had to take him to the hospital last night."

"What happened?" I ask.

"His hand was throbbing," she says. "He had a temperature of 103. The doctor cleaned the wound and removed a lot of dead tissue. She also put him on an intravenous antibiotic."

"What's... that?" Billy asks.

"It's a medicine to fight the infection," Mom says. "It goes into his body through a tube in his arm."

"Is... he... going... to... be... okay?" Billy asks.

"It's a strong antibiotic," Mom says. "The swelling was starting to go down by the time I left.

Hopefully he'll be home by
tomorrow."

Billy puts his head down. He's
crying.

I think about Dad lying in his
hospital bed.

What if the infection gets worse?

LATER. Billy and I wheel our
lawnmower and yard tools down the
block.

"Gilbert," he asks. "What...
about... your... field... trip?"

"It's okay. I know I can't go to
Munson, anyway."

"Where... do... you... want...
to... go?" he asks.

"Raymond State. It's just as
good. And I'll still be able to live
at home."

The truth is that I really want

to go to Munson. But it's seventy-
five miles away, and the living
costs would be too expensive.

Raymond will be the best choice
for me. The programs are just as
good. And it's only five miles away.

We get to the Obert place, our
first job.

Billy starts working on the
flower beds. I start mowing.

It takes about ninety minutes.
After that, we have two more yards
to do.

It's hard not to worry about Dad.
I'm glad we're going to see him
tonight.

HOSPITAL. Dad is asleep when we get
to his room.

He looks weak, like the strength
has drained out of him.

There's a tube in his arm where
the antibiotic goes in.

I look away and try to act like I
don't notice.

Finally, he opens his eyes.

Mom and Billy hug him first.

Then it's my turn. I blink hard
to hold the tears back.

"How was your trip to Munson?"
Dad asks me.

"I decided not to go. Billy and I
did the yard jobs instead."

"But the deadline to apply for
college is November 30," Dad says.
"How will you know where you want to
go?"

It surprises me to hear him say
that. I didn't think he knew about
the deadline.

"It's okay," I say. "I already
know I want to go to Raymond."

The doctor walks in.

"I need to look at your hand,"
she says to Dad. "Should I close the
curtain?"

"You can keep it open," Dad says.
"It's okay for them to see it."

She takes off the bandage. Dad's
hand is puffed up like a balloon.
There's a red slice across his palm
with fluid oozing out.

"It's looking better," the doctor
says. "Can you move your fingers?"

Dad tries. But nothing happens. I
see the frustration on his face.

"You have to be patient," the
doctor says. "It's going to take
time. We have to get the infection
under control."

The nurse puts a new bandage over
the wound and wraps his hand in
gauze.

Dad smiles. But I don't think it's a real smile.

Mom looks worried.

I don't think Dad's hand is going to be okay.

9 CAN'T THINK

MONDAY MORNING. Economics. I take my seat and get ready for class to start. Fiona sits next to me.

"Gilbert, how come you didn't come on the field trip?" she asks.

"I had to do my lawn jobs. My dad was going to take them. But something came up."

"That's too bad," she says. "I think you would have liked it."

I know I would have liked it. But I had to work.

JOURNALISM. Mr. Kennison stands at the door when I get there.

"Gilbert, it was a good trip to Munson State," he says. "What happened?"

"We had a family thing. I had to stay home."

"Have you thought any more about where you want to go?" he asks.

"Raymond State. I think it's the best place for me."

"That's good," he says. "But you need to choose at least two more colleges as backups. Make sure you follow through and get your applications in."

It's easy for him to say that. He doesn't know what it's like.

We only have enough money for me to apply to one college.

FOUR O'CLOCK. I walk out the front door. Ten minutes later, I get to Burger House.

There's a lady at the front counter with red hair.

"Is the manager in?" I ask. "I saw the help-wanted sign."

She reaches under the counter. "Here's an application. Find a table in the back and start filling it out."

I find a spot and begin.

Twenty minutes pass.

I'm surprised when Mr. Rubio sits down across from me.

"Gilbert," he says. "What's going on?"

He's wearing a Burger House uniform. His nametag says he's the assistant manager.

"Mr. Rubio, I didn't know you

worked here."

"I just started," he says. "I've been with the company for sixteen years. They transferred me here last week."

I look around the dining area. It's busy. A lot of people are eating.

"Burger House has been good to me," he says. "I paid my way through college by working here."

He reads my application and frowns. "How come you wrote down that you only want to work during the week?"

"I have lawn jobs that I do on the weekends."

"What's this about metal recycling?"

"I used to help my dad. But we're not doing it anymore."

His eyes peer into me. "I know what that is. My brothers and I did it when I was in school."

It's hard to believe he used to go through trash bins. He knows what I'm going through.

He continues reading the application. Finally, he's done.

"Are you sure you can handle it, going to school, working here, and doing your lawn jobs?"

"I know I can. I have to."

"Why is that?" he asks.

"Our family needs the money."

He looks at me like he's thinking.

"You're hired," he says. "Welcome to Burger House."

EVENING. I sit at the kitchen table to do my homework.

But I can't think.

Mom sits across from me. She adds up numbers on a piece of paper, erases them, writes new numbers, and erases them again.

I see the frustration on her face.

"Mom, what are you working on?" I ask.

"It's our budget," she says. "I have to figure things out because Dad can't work."

"How bad is it?"

"You're old enough now, so you need to know," she says. "We might not be able to make our rent this month."

"Would it help if I got a job?"

"No, it wouldn't," she says. "You already have your yard jobs. You need to focus on school."

I thought she would be happy that
I wanted to work. We need the money,
and I can help.

I go back to my homework.

Mom goes back to her numbers.

I still can't think.

10 PROBABLY

TUESDAY MORNING. Breakfast. Mom, Dad, and Billy are already at the kitchen table when I get there.

I sit down and pour a bowl of cereal. I feel nervous about what I have to say.

"Gilbert," Dad asks. "Is something wrong?"

"I've been thinking about how I can help us."

"What do you mean?" he asks.

"I applied for a job at Burger House. I start after school today."

Mom's eyes get wide. Her face turns red. "I already said you don't need another job."

Billy has a look of panic on his face. He knows how Mom can explode.

"Everything will be okay," I say. "My grades will be under control."

Her face turns redder. "What about your grades? Your future is college, not Burger House."

I knew this would happen. But I'm not going to back down.

I'm relieved when she doesn't say more.

FOUR O'CLOCK. Burger House. I'm ready to start work.

Mr. Rubio motions for me to step behind the counter. He gives me a Burger House shirt to wear.

"We take turns on all the jobs

here," he says. "Today is your day
to work clean-up. You will keep the
tables and floors clean, keep the
parking lot clean, and keep the
bathrooms clean."

Cleanup is not what I wanted.

But at least I'll be making
money.

ONE HOUR LATER. I come out of the
women's restroom with the mop and
bucket.

The front door opens. Some guys
from Edison High School walk in.

One of them is Adam. He's from my
statistics class.

They see me and look at me like
I'm nothing.

I tell myself not to care.

But I do.

I go to the back, put away the

mop and bucket, and come out to
clean tables.

The guys from Edison laugh, spill
soda, and squirt ketchup on the
table.

They make a mess on purpose
because they think they're better
than me.

Finally, they leave.

Mr. Rubio comes out and helps me
clean up.

"I know what you're thinking," he
says. "Try not to let it get to you.
You're better than them."

I know he means well.

But it doesn't help.

HOME. Nine o'clock. I open the front
door and walk in.

I keep thinking about how the
guys from Edison looked at me.

Mom and Dad sit in the living room. I try not to look tired.

"How was work?" Dad asks.

"It was good."

"What did you do?" Mom says.

"I did a lot of different things. It will be good working there."

I'm glad when she doesn't ask more.

I go to the kitchen, make a cup of coffee, and try to forget about the guys from Edison.

I have a lot of homework to do.

ELEVEN O'CLOCK. I'm tired. But I have to keep going.

I click on the Khan Academy to study for the statistics test tomorrow.

Nothing happens.

I look at the internet icon. The

Wi-Fi is off.

I check the router and restart it. Still no internet.

I restart the computer. Still no internet.

I remember last night when Mom was working on the budget.

I wonder if she couldn't pay the internet bill.

I open my statistics book and try to study. I read everything twice and try to do the problems.

But I still can't figure them out.

Dad's hurt. We're broke. And I'm probably going to bomb my statistics test tomorrow.

11 RAYMOND STATE

WEDNESDAY MORNING. Breakfast. I sit across from Mom at the kitchen table.

"Gilbert, I'm sorry about the internet," Mom says. "I didn't have a choice. There was nothing I could do."

I get up and take my dishes to the sink. "That's okay," I say. "I'll figure it out."

What I really mean is that I stayed up past midnight to study for the statistics test today.

I'm dead tired.

I tried my hardest.

But I still don't know it.

LUNCH. I skip eating and go straight
to the library. Maybe I can get on
the Khan Academy.

There's an empty computer in the
back. But when I get there, it's out
of order.

All of the other computers are
being used. Some of the kids play
video games on them.

It makes me mad. And it's against
the rules.

But I would never snitch.

STATISTICS. I take my seat and get
ready for the test.

Adam sits to my left. I see a
folded-up piece of paper in his

palm.

It's a cheat sheet.

He gives me a dirty look and closes his hand.

I thought he was smart.

But I was wrong.

He's a cheater.

The bell rings to begin class. Mr. Braden comes to the front and starts handing out the tests.

"Read the questions carefully," he says. "Keep your eyes on your own papers. Good luck."

He always says good luck. I know he means it.

But today, it makes me feel worse.

I look at the first problem. I don't know how to do it. The rest of the problems also look bad.

Twenty minutes pass. Mr. Braden

walks up behind Adam.

"What's that in your hand?" he asks.

"Nothing."

"Let me see."

Adam opens his hand and gives him the cheat sheet.

Mr. Braden frowns and marks an X across the front of Adam's test paper.

I want to smile. But I look down and act like I'm working.

It feels great to see Adam get caught.

CLASS ENDS. I leave statistics and go into the hallway.

Adam comes up and gets in my face.

"You're a punk," he says. "You told Mr. Braden what I was doing."

I step forward to face him. "What was that?"

He balls up his fists like he's going to hit me.

I get ready to fight.

He walks away.

HOME. It's late. I sit at the kitchen table and begin my homework.

I wish I could go to bed. But I have to keep trying.

Mom and Dad talk in the living room. Their voices are low, but I can hear what they say.

"I know you don't like it," Mom says. "But at least the infection is getting better."

"I know," says Dad. "But what am I supposed to do if I can't move my fingers?"

"Have you thought any more about

signing up for adult school?" Mom
asks.

"I don't know if I can take it,"
Dad says. "It was bad enough going
to school when I was a kid."

I finish economics and begin my
homework for physics.

It's a required class for
college. But with no internet and no
Khan Academy, it's a lot harder.

Raymond State College is getting
farther and farther away.

12 HANG MY HEAD

THURSDAY MORNING. Edison High School. I enter the front gate and turn left to go to my locker.

Everyone looks happy.

I wish I could feel that way.

I see my locker and stop. Somebody wrote SNITCH across it with a black marker.

It had to be Adam.

I'm tired of him and the way he thinks he's better than me.

I know what I have to do.

LUNCH. I stand by the drinking
fountain. From here, I can see
everybody in the food court.

There he is, Adam.

He walks to get in line.

I step in front of him to block
his way.

"You're a punk," I say.

"You're a snitch."

I swing hard and hit him in the
jaw.

His head snaps back.

Somebody grabs me from behind.

DEANS' OFFICE. Mr. Wiley hangs up
his phone and looks hard at me.

"Gilbert, you really messed up,"
he says. "You're getting five days
of in-school suspension. You might
also be getting a citation for
battery."

"What does that mean?"

"It means that you will get a
police record. You will have to go
to court. And you could go to jail."

"But I only hit him once."

"That's all it took," Mr. Wiley
says. "He lost a tooth."

There's a knock on the door.

Officer Krebb, the school police
officer, comes in and sits across
from me.

I try not to shake.

"You're lucky," says Officer
Krebb. "Adam's parents said no to
pressing charges. But you will still
have to pay his dental bills. They
are probably going to be a lot."

I hang my head.

What have I done?

13 FIND A WAY

BURGER HOUSE. Late afternoon. I sit across from Mr. Rubio at a table in the back. Nobody else can hear us.

"Gilbert, what happened?" he asks.

"I couldn't take it anymore. He wrote SNITCH across my locker."

Mr. Rubio shakes his head. "What were you thinking? Did you make things better by hitting him?"

I think about Dad with his hand messed up.

I think about Mom trying to

figure out our budget.

I think about Billy and how he looks up to me.

"You messed up bad," Mr. Rubio says. "But you're going to get through this."

I look out the window. I don't see how I can.

"First, you have to apologize," Mr. Rubio says. "You will write apology letters to your parents, to Adam, and to the principal. You will also be doing cleanup here for the next ten days. You have to think about what you are doing, not act like a little kid."

THIRTY MINUTES LATER. I finish my first apology letter and read it one more time. I hope it's good enough.

Dear Mom and Dad,

     I know I messed up bad. I wish I
could take back everything I did.
I'm sorry for hitting Adam.
     I've always wanted to be
somebody. I want to go to college
and be a teacher someday. I want to
do something to help kids. I want to
be someone that Billy can look up
to.
     I know it's not enough to say
that I'm sorry. And I don't know if
I can make it up to you.
     But I'm going to keep trying to
make things right and make you proud
of me.

Your son,
Gilbert

SIXTY MINUTES PASS. My letters are done. Mr. Rubio sits across from me and begins reading. Finally, he finishes.

"I know that things have been hard for you," he says. "You've hit a lot of roadblocks. But you can't let them stop you. You have to find a way to get around them and keep going."

I think about his words.

I was stupid to hit Adam.

I have to find a way to come back from this.

14 ONE WEEK LATER

FRIDAY MORNING. Edison High School.
I walk through the front gate.

My in-school suspension is over.
I'll be back in my real classes
again.

But I'm lost even more in
statistics. And we're having a test
today.

I get to my locker. Fiona comes
over.

"Gilbert, I'm glad you're back,"
she says. "You missed a lot in
statistics. Let me know if you need

help getting caught up."

She gives me a piece of paper with her phone number.

"Just call me," she says.

It's nice of her to do that.

But the test is today.

ECONOMICS. Mr. Rubio comes to the front of the classroom.

"Don't forget," he says. "Your applications are due on Monday for the state college system. I want all of you to apply somewhere."

I feel good.

My application for Raymond State is ready.

Mr. Rubio said he would check it tonight at Burger House.

STATISTICS. Mr. Braden comes to the front of the classroom.

"Some of you have been falling behind," he says. "But if you've been paying attention and doing your homework, this should be an easy test for you."

Fiona smiles. I know she's going to get an A.

"Keep using the Khan Academy," Mr. Braden says. "You should also find a study partner. And I'm here after school to help you."

He hands out the test papers. I skim the questions to see what I know.

I thought it would be bad.

And it is.

I do my best and try to solve the problems.

But I can only do some of them.

The two weeks of school I missed because of the concussion and in-

school suspension are really hurting
me.

JOURNALISM. Fiona's desk is next to
mine. She smiles when I sit down.

Mr. Kennison comes to the front
of the classroom.

"How many of you have completed
an application for the state college
system?" he asks.

Everybody raises their hand. Mine
will be done tonight, so I raise my
hand, too.

Fiona comes up next to me when
class is over.

"Where did you apply?" she asks.

"Raymond State."

"Anywhere else?"

"No, just Raymond. What about
you?"

"I applied to Munson State," she

says. "I also applied to Brown University and Stanford. My first choice is Stanford."

That's great for her.

But it makes me feel worse about myself.

BURGER HOUSE. My shift ends. I find a table in the back and turn on my laptop.

The application for Raymond State is ready.

Mr. Rubio comes back to look it over. He smiles when he reads the essay section.

"Gilbert, this application is excellent," he says. "You should be proud."

He shakes my hand and returns to the front of the restaurant.

This is it. My dream. It's really

happening.

The last step is to pay the application fee. I put in Mom's credit card number and click send.

Nothing happens. The website says there's an error.

I check the card number and try again. It still doesn't work.

I try again, again, and again.

Then it hits me. Mom must have maxed out her credit card.

I bet it's because she had to pay Adam's dental bill.

All of my work has been for nothing.

I close the laptop and walk out the back door.

I don't want Mr. Rubio to see the look on my face.

15 ON MY WAY

TUESDAY. Journalism. I take my seat and wish I was somewhere else.

The deadline has passed. The last day to apply for a state college was yesterday.

Mr. Kennison comes to the front of the classroom.

"Going to college next year will be a big step in your lives," he says. "I'm excited about what lies ahead for you."

I wish I could feel the same. College does not lie ahead for me.

"I'm going to pass out some blank index cards," he says. "When you get your card, write down the names of the colleges where you have applied. This is anonymous, so do not write your name."

I get my card and look around the room. Everyone is smiling and excited.

I write NOWHERE on my card, turn it face down, and give it to Mr. Kennison when he comes by my desk.

He shuffles the cards and reads off the colleges where people have applied.

Everyone seems happy.

But I feel worse.

AFTER SCHOOL. I walk home with Billy.

Usually, he's happy when school

lets out. But not today.

"Did something happen?" I ask.

"This... morning... you... said... you... were... not... going... to... college."

"It will be okay," I say. "Lots of people don't go to college."

"You... always... told... me... never... to... give... up... What... about... you?"

He doesn't know what I've been through.

I'm tired of getting knocked down all the time.

College is not for me.

BURGER HOUSE. My shift is done. I sit in the back and turn on my laptop.

I have statistics to do. But I get on the Raymond State website

instead. The campus is beautiful.
And they have a great teacher-
education program.

Mr. Rubio comes over and sits
across from me.

"Gilbert, are you excited about
Raymond State?" he asks.

"I didn't apply."

The smile leaves his face. "What
happened?"

"I decided it's not the right
time for me. I'm going to sit out a
year to make money."

"But I watched you apply on
Friday," he says.

"The website wouldn't accept my
application. My mom's credit card
was maxed out. Everything will be
better if I sit out next year."

"Why don't you apply to Jasper?"
he asks. "The application is free."

"I've always wanted to go to a four-year school. I think it will be better if I wait."

"I went to Jasper, and it was great," he says. "I worked part-time at Burger House and got my associate's degree. Then I went to Raymond State and got my bachelor's degree. You could do the same."

I wish he would leave me alone. My mind is made up.

"Let me see your computer," he says.

I slide it across to him and watch as he types. He turns it around so I can see the screen.

It's the Jasper Community College website. There's a list of programs they offer. One of them is teacher education.

"Remember what I told you," he

says. "Don't let the roadblocks stop you. Find a way around them and keep going. I know you want to be a teacher. This will help you get there."

He stands and goes back to work.

I look at the application.

I think about what Billy said.

I think about how I've always wanted to be a teacher.

I put in my information and apply.

HOME. It's ten-thirty when I open the front door. Mom and Dad sit in the living room.

"How was work?" Dad asks.

"It was fine."

"You never mentioned your application for Raymond State," Mom says. "How did it go?"

I take a breath. "I tried to apply on Friday. But the website wouldn't accept your credit card. I decided to sit out a year."

Mom's face turns red.

Dad looks mad. "Why didn't you tell us? Maybe we could have done something."

"It's going to be okay," I say. "Mr. Rubio talked to me. I put in my application for Jasper Community College. They have a good program for future teachers."

Mom and Dad smile.

I feel better now.

It's been hard.

But I'm on my way.

16 OTHER SIDE

WEDNESDAY MORNING. Edison High School. I walk through the front gate.

Everything seems better today. Jasper Community College is going to be good for me. I have a future now.

Fiona is there when I get to my locker.

"Gilbert, you look happy," she says.

"It's a long story," I say. "But things are looking up. Can I still call you to get help with

85

statistics?"

"Of course," she says. "Any time
is fine."

Things are getting better now.

With Fiona helping me, I think I
have a chance to pass statistics.

AFTER LUNCH. I walk to statistics.
Fiona and Lacey walk in front of me.
They don't know I'm behind them.

"Did you hear about Terrence?"
Lacey asks. "I heard he's going to
Jasper."

"That's a surprise," Fiona says.
"I thought he was smarter than
that."

Fiona's words hit hard. What will
she think of me?

"You know how it is," Lacey says.
"He lives on the other side of the
train bridge."

I wait for Fiona to say something back.

But she doesn't.

Lacey laughs that stupid laugh of hers.

I stop and watch them walk away.

I should have known.

STATISTICS. Mr. Braden comes to the front of the classroom. He's going to give us one of his pep talks.

"I know that some of you have been having problems in this class," he says. "But don't give up. Keep trying and keep going. I'm serious when I say that every single one of you can pass this class."

I feel Fiona looking at me.

I make sure I keep looking straight ahead.

I don't need statistics to get

into Jasper.

And I don't need her.

AFTER SCHOOL. Billy and I walk home.

"You... seem... down," Billy
says. "What's... wrong?"

"I was excited about going to
Jasper. But now, I'm not so sure."

"Why?" he asks.

"Just something I heard today."

Fiona's words come back to me.
She thinks I'm stupid.

We pass under the train bridge.

I feel better when we get to the
other side.

17 MAYBE

THURSDAY MORNING. School starts in twenty minutes.

I go to my locker to get my economics book.

There she is, Fiona. It looks like she's waiting for me.

I turn around and walk the other way.

I don't want to see her after what she said yesterday.

In fact, I don't even want to think about her.

STATISTICS. Mr. Braden passes out the review sheets for our test tomorrow.

I look at mine. None of it makes sense. There's no way I'll be able to pass the test.

Mr. Braden begins speaking. "The test tomorrow will count double toward your report-card grade. If your other scores have been low, this will be a chance to bring yourself up."

I know the test can help me. But it's a lost cause. I'm too far behind.

Fiona reaches over and drops a folded-up piece of paper on my desk.

It's a note.

I feel like throwing it away.

But I decide to read it later.

JOURNALISM. I get to my seat and
open Fiona's note.

Dear Gilbert,

*You act like you hate me. But I
don't know what I've done.*

*When you got hurt in the truck
crash, I was worried.*

*And when you got suspended, I was
even more worried.*

*You are a special person. I hope
you will let me help you.*

Fiona

I fold up the note and put it in
my pocket.

She's probably looking at me. I
make sure I don't look at her.

BURGER HOUSE. I finish my shift and find a table in the back where I can do my homework.

I need to study for the statistics test tomorrow.

But I'm still lost.

I take out the review sheet and turn on my laptop.

Maybe there's something on the Khan Academy that will help me.

THIRTY MINUTES PASS. I'm still studying for the statistics test.

The Khan Academy is helping. But the two weeks of class I missed are really hurting me.

The front door opens.

Fiona walks in.

She comes over and sits across from me.

"Gilbert, are you studying for

the test tomorrow?"

I want her to leave. But I don't know how to say it.

She looks at the review sheet. "Which question are you working on?"

"Number one."

"Can I help?"

I know I need it. I have to say something. "Okay," I tell her.

We go to the first question. She takes her time and explains how to do it.

Now, I understand.

We go to the next question, the next, and the next.

I understand everything. She makes it seem easy.

I look at my watch. It's after ten.

"Can I give you a ride home?" she asks.

I'm not sure if I want her to see where I live. But the ride will help.

"Sure," I say. "Thanks."

We leave and walk out to the parking lot.

She reaches out to hold my hand.

Maybe I was wrong about her.

18 FUTURE NOW

FRIDAY MORNING. I get to my locker. It feels great to see Fiona.

"Gilbert, are you ready for the test?" she asks.

"I think so. I got up early and studied again this morning. I still remember everything you showed me."

She smiles and touches my arm.

I wonder if she would go out with me.

STATISTICS. Mr. Braden comes to the front of the classroom.

"Clear your desks for the test,"
he says.

My hands shake when I get my test
paper. But when I look at the first
question, I know I can do it.

I skim the rest of the questions.
I know I can do them, too.

I complete the first problem, the
next, and the next.

When I turn in my paper, I feel
good about my answers on all of
them.

It's like a load has been lifted
off my shoulders.

AFTERNOON. I walk home with Billy. I
haven't felt this good about school
in a long time.

"You... seem... happy," Billy
says.

"I think I aced my statistics

test. I finally understand what I'm doing."

"You... didn't... give... up," he says. "I... knew... you... could... do... it."

He doesn't say much. But his words mean a lot to me.

BURGER HOUSE. Break time. I sit in the back and take a bite out of my hamburger.

Mr. Rubio comes over and sits across from me.

"You impressed me last night when you were studying with that girl," he says. "I could tell by the look on your face that you were all business."

"She was helping me with statistics. We had a test today. I think I might get an A or a B."

"Remember what you did to make that happen," he says. "You worked hard and didn't give up. It will help you at Jasper. And it will help you the rest of your life."

TEN O'CLOCK. I open the front door. I'm tired from work and school. But I'm happy.

Mom and Dad are sitting at the kitchen table when I get inside.

"How was school today?" Mom asks.

"I think I might get an A or a B on my statistics test today."

"That's great," Mom says. "Guess what else happened."

Dad smiles and shows me a letter. It's from Edison Adult School.

"I start next week," he says. "I'm going back to get my high school diploma."

I think about our nights
collecting cans together.
     That was all he could do.
     But the look in his eyes says
everything.
     We both have a future now.

19   FIFTEEN YEARS LATER

THURSDAY NIGHT. I pull over to the curb in front of Edison High School.

Dad gets in with his briefcase and closes the door. "Gilbert, thanks for picking me up."

"No problem," I say. "How soon before your car gets out of the shop?"

"About two more days. The damage was worse than it looked."

I turn the corner. We go down Glendon Street.

"Remember when you wrecked the

truck here?" Dad asks.

"I remember the accident. But the truck was a wreck the day you bought it."

"Just drive," Dad says. "And try not to hit any trees."

We pass under the train bridge to go home.

"Dad, how are your classes?" I ask.

"Pretty good," he says.

"How are the students doing?"

"Their skills are getting better," Dad says. "One man is forty years old. He reminds me of me when I was learning to read."

We stop at the red light on Jupiter Street.

"How's Fiona?" Dad asks.

"Pretty good," I say. "She's done with her morning sickness."

I continue driving. It's hard to believe we're going to have a second child.

TEN MINUTES LATER. I park in the driveway and walk up the steps to our front door.

The house is quiet when I get inside. Shelly is fast asleep.

Fiona grades papers at the kitchen table. She smiles when I sit across from her.

"Today was a big day for Shelly," Fiona says. "Your mom told me she was stacking her blocks. She wasn't just knocking them down."

I think about the day Shelly was born. I remember how worried I was. But everything turned out fine.

Now she's two. She's growing so fast.

I open my briefcase and begin
reading the essays from my tenth-
grade English class.

I asked the students to write
about their dreams after high
school.

I think about Mr. Rubio and what
he said fifteen years ago.

He must have told us a hundred
times that we could achieve our
dreams.

I didn't know if I could believe
it back then.

But I do now.

20 MORE THAN RIGHT

FRIDAY MORNING. Edison High School. I stand at the door and say hi to the students as they walk into my tenth-grade English class.

Vance comes in. He's been here a week.

I know from his address that he lives on the other side of the train bridge.

He never says anything. It's like he wants to be invisible.

The bell rings. I go to the front of the classroom. "When you write your essays today, the important thing is to relax. Pretend you're talking to one of your friends."

I walk around the classroom and watch the students as they work.

Vance is having a hard time. I think back to when I was in his shoes.

I kneel by his desk to help him. I can feel the effort he is making.

AFTER SCHOOL. I sit at my desk, checking papers. I'm surprised when Vance walks in.

He shows me his essay again.

"I worked on it during lunch," he says. "Is it any better?"

I read the essay and feel myself smiling.

"Nice job," I say. "This is a big improvement."

His face lights up. "Guess what?"
he says. "I got a job at Burger
House."

"No kidding," I say. "Who hired
you?"

"His name is Mr. Billy. He's the
manager."

"You know what?" I say. "He's my
cousin."

Vance's mouth drops open. "I
start next Tuesday. I'll be working
twenty hours a week."

"I worked there too when I was
going here," I say. "My boss was Mr.
Rubio."

"The teacher?" he asks.

"Yep, that's him."

He leaves my classroom with a
smile on his face. Things are
getting better for him.

FOUR O'CLOCK. I pack up my briefcase and leave my room.

Mr. Rubio's classroom is at the end of the hall. He's still at his desk when I get there.

"One of my kids starts at Burger House next week," I say.

Mr. Rubio smiles. "I still remember the look on your face when I gave you clean-up on your first day. It was hard for me not to laugh. But you learned from it."

"I still remember what you said to me. You told me to keep trying and not let the roadblocks stop me."

"Was I right?" he asks.

"You were more than right."

ACKNOWLEDGMENTS

I would like to express my sincere appreciation to everyone who gave me feedback while I was writing this book.

COFFEE HOUSE WRITERS GROUP: Noemi Arellano-Summer, Paul Bello, Luke Casipe, Rose Chang, Nicholas Chiazza, Nick Cruz, Sukie Fogg, Steve Hovland, Darian Lane, John Lowell, Ani Minasian, Jean Pliska, Mark Yang, Ron Wolff, and Min.

SOCIETY OF CHILDREN'S BOOK WRITERS AND ILLUSTRATORS: Jemisco Chambers-Black, Sarah Daniels, Carlene Griffith, Karena Hamilton, Christine Henderson, Erin Lagerberg, Toni Momberger, Molly O'Neill, Jennifer

Parsons, Kelly Powers, Kaitlyn
Sanchez, Desi St. Amat, Liz Turney,
Samantha Winkler, and Joyce Wyels.

SOUTHERN CALIFORNIA WRITERS
CONFERENCE: Cherie Kephart, Jennifer
Silva Redmond, and Robert Yehling.

Thank you, Pam Sheppard, for your
advice on creating this series.

Thank you, Laura Perkins, for your
feedback and careful editing.

Thank you, Betty Jean, for your
feedback, your wisdom, your love,
and for being my wife.

ABOUT THE AUTHOR

My dream of becoming a writer started at Whitworth College. I was lucky to have a teacher, Dr. Tammy Reid, who believed in me and encouraged me. After college, I began a career as an educator, teaching reading and English at a middle school in Los Angeles. I went to college at night to earn a doctorate in education. I then served as a high-school principal and district administrator. One of the most important things I have learned is that everyone can achieve success. Set your sights high, work hard, and never give up. Strive to be the best that you can be.

FINDING FORWARD BOOKS

At Finding Forward Books, we publish short novels for reluctant teen readers that show teens overcoming challenges in their lives. Our goal is for students to improve their reading skills, develop positive attitudes, and increase their success in school.

The books are suitable for all students, including English Learners and those with learning disabilities. Lexile measures range from 390 to 560.

The books have been praised in *Kirkus Reviews*, *Publishers Weekly BookLife Reviews*, *Foreword Clarion Reviews*, and *BlueInk Reviews*.

ADDITIONAL TITLES

TAKEN AWAY. A teen must adapt after his dad is sent to prison.

NO PLACE TO HIDE. A discouraged tenth grader improves his reading skills.

NEVER WANTED. A neglected teen is placed in a foster home.

ALL ALONE. A teen learns to cope with his mom's alcoholism.

KNOCKED DOWN. A football player learns the importance of honesty.

OVERSPRAY. A teen experiences grief after his father dies.

TORN. A student with everything
learns to care about a student who
has nothing.

BLUE WALL. A troubled teen battles
back from depression.

LETTERZ. A teen struggling with
dyslexia strives to succeed in high
school.

FINDING HOME. A homeless teen works
to build a better life for himself.

Finding Forward Books
Short Novels for Teens About
Issues Faced by Teens
www.findingforwardbooks.com